Best Wishes

2017

Music makes pictures and often tells stories, all of it magic and all of it true. And all of the pictures and ...agic, the music is you.

Guest Dedication

This is John's most celebrated song worldwide and his first number one hit. An anthem not only to West Virginia, but to the world. A song that will be played and remembered forever. — Hal Thau, John Denver's manager

Illustrator's Dedication

For the Rammell, Glenn, Sigler, Klinger, Amnah and Murphy families—thank you for an upbringing filled with love and music. — C.C.

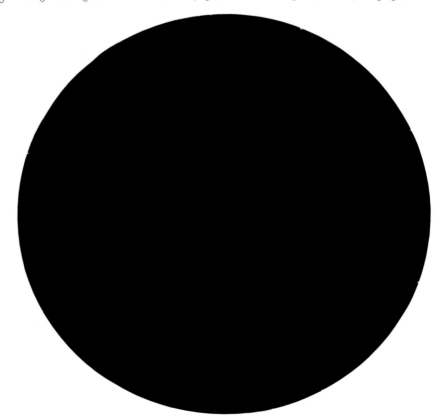

ACKNOWLEDGEMENTS BY THE PUBLISHER

John Denver's
Take Me Home, Country Roads

FAMILY ♥ REUNION

Adapted and Illustrated by Christopher Canyon
DAWN PUBLICATIONS

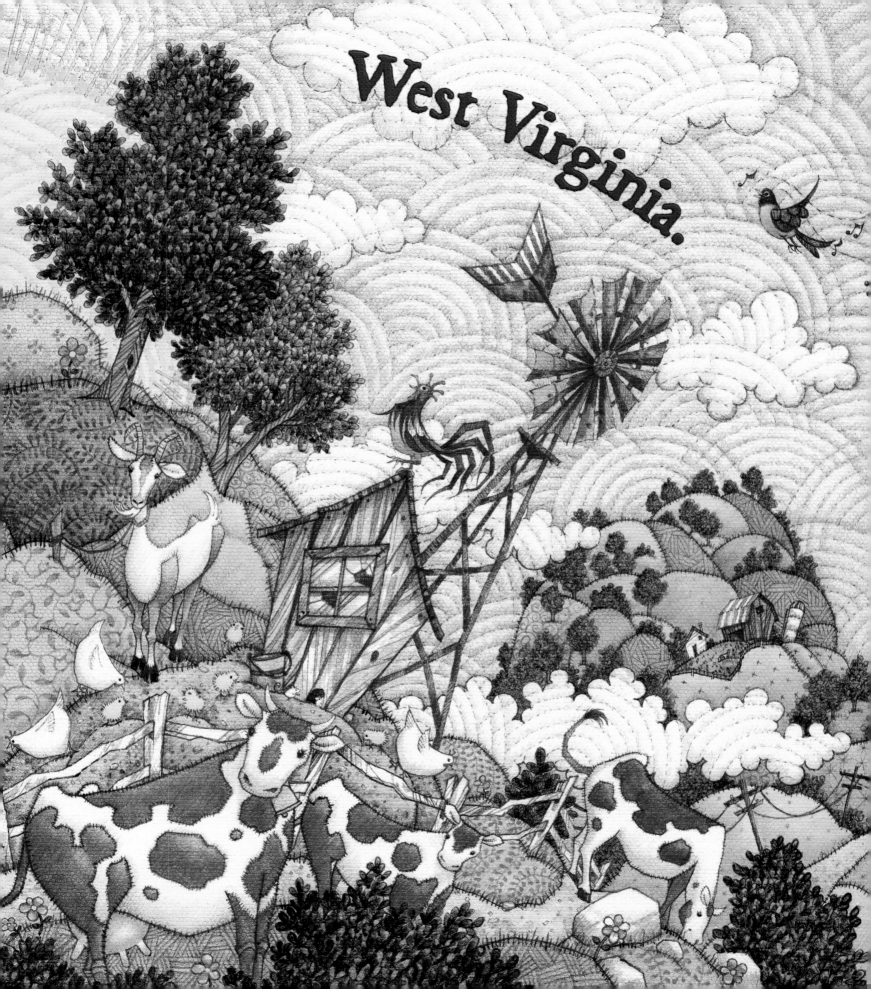

West Virginia.

Blue Ridge Mountains,

Life is old there,
older than the trees,

West Virginia, mountain momma, take me home, country roads.

All my memories, gather 'round her.

MUD CREEK COAL MINE

Miner's lady, stranger to blue water.

painted on the sky,

And drivin' down the road I get a feelin'
that I should have been home yesterday.

Country roads, take me home,
to the place, I belong.

West Virginia, mountain momma, take me home, country roads.

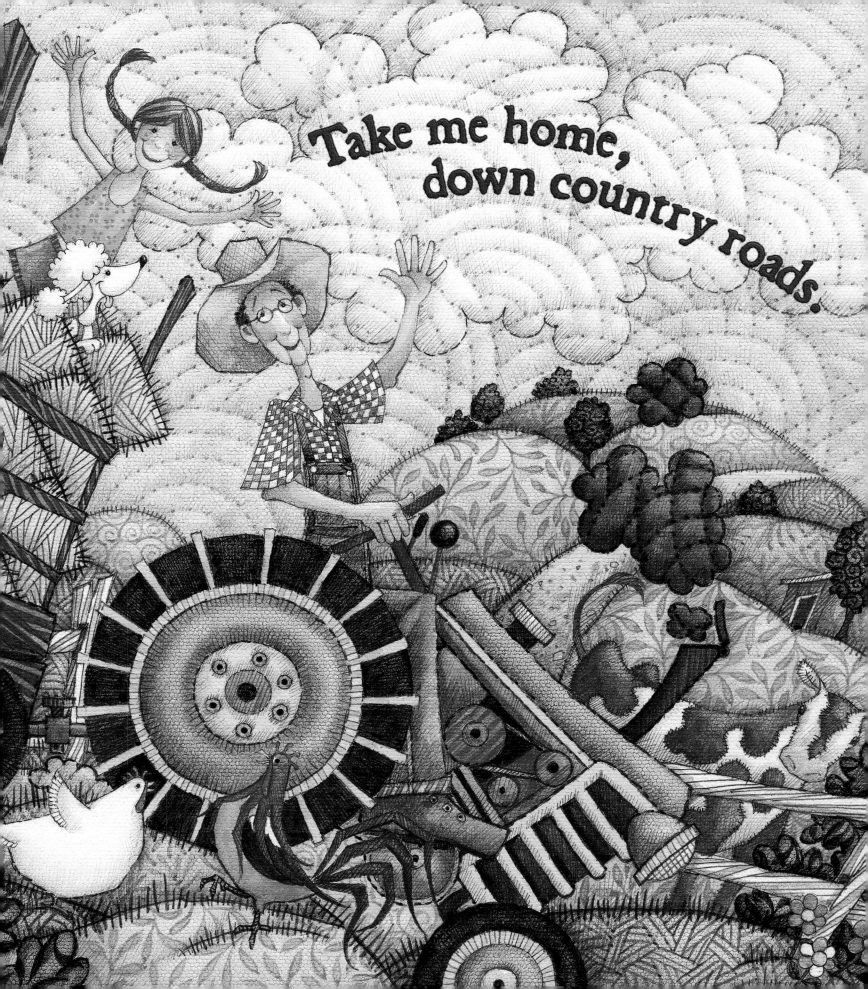

This great song began with a drive to a family reunion. A couple of musical friends of John's, Bill Danoff and Taffy Nivert, were driving along Clopper Road in Maryland, heading for her family reunion near Gaithersburg. They were captivated by the beauty of the rolling hills. Before long they started humming a tune and putting words to it. But they couldn't quite finish it.

Soon afterwards, John was singing at a nightclub in Washington, D.C. After the show John and Annie Denver arrived at Bill and Taffy's basement apartment. They were very late—it was 3 a.m., because their car had been involved in a minor accident, and John had one thumb in a cast and couldn't play guitar. Bill and Taffy shared their half-finished song with John. John was ecstatic: "That's a hit, let's finish it!" By 6 a.m., "Take Me Home, Country Roads" was born—and set in West Virginia.

The very next night they performed it together at the nightclub, and the place went crazy. It seemed as though the audience would never stop applauding. The next week John recorded it in New York, and "Country Roads" became John's first big hit. In 1999 it received one of ten awards as a "Country Song of the Century."

John was continually inspired by nature. He wrote "Sunshine On My Shoulders" on a dreary Minnesota day in late winter, appreciating in its absence the beauty of sunshine. He wrote "Perhaps Love" on a drive along the California coast. The chorus of "Calypso" came to him "almost in the time it takes to say it" while on board Jacque Cousteau's famous ship by that name. He wrote "Annie's Song" on a ski lift, in the ten minutes it took to go from the bottom to the top of the mountain. As his daughter, Anna Kate, has said: "My Dad was thrilled by life, so often struck by how amazing or how beautiful the world could be. He was tickled by the smallest things, overjoyed with new experiences, and never ceased to be captivated by the completely routine appearance of the sun or the stars."

Christopher Canyon did not know that the song originated with an actual family reunion. He just conceived of it that way—and, after the project was almost finished, found out how intuitive he was! In his youth, Christopher was deeply touched by John Denver. "John's songs gave me hope, joy, and an unbounded belief in possibilities," he says.

Christopher is an award winning artist, musician and performer dedicated to sharing the joy and importance of the arts with children, educators and families. He frequently visits schools, providing entertaining and educational programs and is a popular speaker at conferences throughout the country. "Everyone has what it takes to be artistic, and it's not talent. It is our creativity," he says. "As humans we are all creative beings and our individual creativity is one of our most powerful gifts. If we celebrate and use our creativity it is amazing how much we can learn, how much we can discover and how much joy we have."

This is the ninth book Christopher Canyon has illustrated for Dawn Publications, including the earlier books in the "John Denver & Kids" series. He lives in historic German Village in Columbus, Ohio with his artist wife Jeanette Canyon, also a children's book illustrator.

ALSO IN THE JOHN DENVER & KIDS BOOK SERIES

Sunshine On My Shoulders
Ancient Rhymes: A Dolphin Lullaby
Grandma's Feather Bed

Countrywide Publications

Bill Danoff, Taffy Nivert, and John Denver in concert.

Dawn Publications is dedicated to inspiring in children a deeper understanding and appreciation for all life on Earth. Some titles present particular animals, habitats or aspects of nature; others focus on more universal qualities. In each case, our purpose is to encourage a life-long bond with the natural world. To review our titles or to order, please visit us at www.dawnpub.com, or call 800-545-7475.

Take Me Home, Country Roads

Words and Music by
John Denver, Bill Danoff and Taffy Nivert